For Daisy Brooks
J.W.

For Jackie, my little star
P.D.

ORCHARD BOOKS
338 Euston Road,
London NW1 3BH
Orchard Books Australia
Hachette Children's Books
Level 17/207 Kent Street, Sydney, NSW 2000

First published in Great Britain in 2005
First paperback publication in 2006

Text © Jeanne Willis 2005
Illustrations © Penny Dann 2005

A CIP catalogue record for this book is available from the British Library.

ISBN 1 84616 058 8

1 3 5 7 9 10 8 6 4 2

Printed in Singapore

The Secret Fairy

The Talent Show

Jeanne Willis & Penny Dann

ORCHARD BOOKS

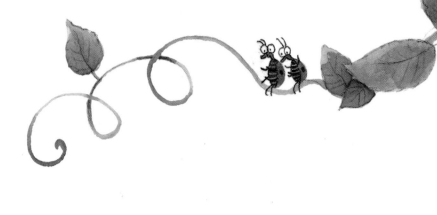

In Secret Fairyland, everyone was fluttering with excitement. The Fairy Queen was holding a Talent Show.

The Fairy Queen's TALENT SHOW This Saturday. All Welcome!

Lovely Shoes

FAIRY CAKES

Blossom and her Secret Fairy friends couldn't wait to put their acts together.

Blossom was going to play
her daffodil trumpet.

'Lovely!' said Lavender.
'You play so sweetly –
not at all like a foghorn.'

Lavender thought she'd
make up a flower dance.

'You must!' said Hollyhock.
'You're so graceful, like petals
wafting in a breeze.'

Hollyhock wanted to sing but couldn't think of a song.
'How about Mary, Mary?' said Nettle.
'It's the Fairy Queen's favourite.'

It was a great idea . . .

. . . unlike Nettle's decision to juggle eggs!

Eggs for Sale

'You're very brave,'
said Blossom.

It seemed as if everyone had
a talent except for Bluebell.

'There is one thing I'm good at,'
she said. 'Being beautiful!'

Only it wasn't a Beauty Competition –
so what could she do?

Blossom offered to
teach her a magic trick.

'Thank you!' said Bluebell.
'The Fairy Queen likes
magic, doesn't she?'

'Of course she does,' laughed Blossom.
'She loves magic!'

While the fairies were practising for
the show, along came the Tricksy Pixies.
'Let us watch. We'll be ever so good,
won't we, Tansy?' said Teasel.

'We'll be as good as gold,
Teasel,' said Tansy.

'Oh no, you won't!' said Blossom.
'Oh yes, we will!' they said.
So the Secret Fairies let them stay . . .

Blossom knew her music off by heart.
Lavender had learnt her dance steps.

But Hollyhock was
in a terrible tizzy.

She was afraid she'd forget her words,
so Blossom wrote them down:

Mary, Mary, quite contrary,
    How does your garden grow?
With silver bells and cockle shells
    And pretty maids all in a row.

Then Bluebell had one last practice of her magic scarf trick. She put six scarves into a hat, waved her wand and, hey presto, the scarves joined together!

Nettle was so amazed she dropped her eggs.

'Oh, bumblebees! What a mess. Now what am I going to do?' she squealed.

Bluebell looked at
the Dandelion Clock.

It was time for the fairies
to go and get ready for the show.
'But I have to clean up this egg yolk!' sighed Nettle.
'Don't worry, we'll clean it up!' said Tansy and Teasel.

And they promised to pack everything
the fairies needed for the show and fly it to
the palace on Snapdragon, their dragonfly.

The fairies were ever so grateful.
'Maybe the Tricksy Pixies aren't
so tricksy after all,' thought Blossom.

The fairies flew to Bluebell's Beauty Parlour
to change into their outfits . . .

. . . and have their hair done.

At last, the Secret Fairies
were on their way in
a Busy Bees taxi . . .

. . . and they arrived
at the palace.
'We can't wait to see
you perform!' said Tansy.
'We've put all your stuff
backstage,' said Teasel.

The show was about
to start.

Stage
Door

The curtain began to rise.
The Secret Fairies were
shaking with excitement.
'Good luck, Blossom!' they whispered.
Blossom played her trumpet
for the Fairy Queen.

But it made the most awful noise!
Something was stuck inside it.
She blew hard . . .

...POOT!

Out shot Fuzzy Caterpillar!

'How did he get there?' gasped Blossom.

'I don't know!' giggled Teasel. 'Do you, Tansy?'

It was Lavender's turn to dance.
She curtsied beautifully to the Fairy Queen.
But suddenly, she felt itchy all over and
leapt about like a startled frog.

'Anyone would think she had Tickle
Powder in her tutu,' said Teasel.
'Who'd do a terrible thing like that,
Teasel?' teased Tansy.

Bluebell's trick didn't go very well either.
There were meant to be scarves in the hat.

But when she said the magic word
and pulled them out, they weren't
scarves at all – they were . . .

'KNICKERS!'
tittered Teasel.

Hollyhock grabbed her song
sheet and started to sing:

'Hairy fairy in the dairy,

Cows in your garden moo,

With rusty bells and cow pat smells

The whole place stinks of . . . ?'

'These are the wrong words!' she wailed.

'You're right!' roared
Teasel and Tansy.

'I will save the show with my juggling skills!' said Nettle. But when she reached inside her bag of eggs . . .

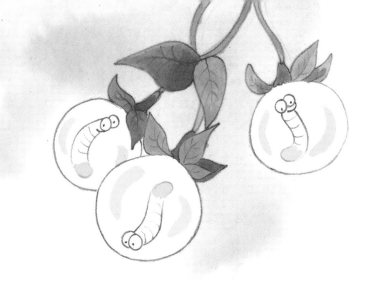

Ouch!

Ouch!

Ouch!

Someone had swapped them for prickly conkers!

'Wasn't me – it was Tansy!' said Teasel.

'Wasn't me – it was Teasel!' said Tansy.

'You Tricksy Pixies! The Queen will never ask us to the palace again!' said Blossom.

But the Fairy Queen was clapping and cheering! 'Bravo!' she said. 'That was the funniest show ever! You are all so talented.'

And everyone won a bag of Royal Fairy Dust.

All except two.
'Not fair!' stamped Teasel.
'We helped those goody-goody
fairies win,' stomped Tansy.
'We want some Royal Fairy Dust too.'

To their great surprise, Blossom gave them hers.
'They don't deserve it!' said Nettle.
'Oh, I think they do,' Blossom smiled.

Soon, the Tricksy Pixies were itching all over.
'Boo! This isn't Royal Fairy Dust, is it, Teasel?'
scratched Tansy.

'No, Tansy, it isn't!' scritched Teasel.
'Blossom gave us Tickle Powder instead!'
'Let's say sorry to the Secret Fairies!'
said Tansy. 'Or they'll banish us forever!'

'Tansy is sorry,'
said Teasel.

'Teasel is sorry,'
said Tansy.

And they promised never to be tricksy again.

'But I think they're telling fairy stories,' laughed Blossom. 'Don't you?'